Patrick the Pup

Sheila Black

Illustrated by Scott Ross

Ariel Books ✦ Andrews and McMeel ✦ Kansas City

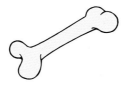

Patrick the Pup is a registered trademark of F.A.O. Schwarz.

Designed by: Junie Lee

Colorized by: Christy Truxaw

ISBN: 0-8362-2113-3

Library of Congress Catalog Card Number: 96-84508

Patrick the Pup

Patrick was a little, furry, brown puppy.
He had big, round eyes, floppy ears,
and a waggy tail.

One sunny morning Patrick ran outside.
He wanted to play. But he had no one
to play with. Suddenly . . .

he spotted a yellow butterfly.
"Hello, butterfly," he barked.
"Will you play with me?"

"Sure. Let's fly from flower to flower!"
The butterfly rose into the sky.

Patrick tried to follow. Up he jumped
as high as he could but . . .

Oh, no! Down he tumbled onto his little,
black nose. When he got up again,
the butterfly had flown away.

Then Patrick spotted a green frog
sitting at the edge of a pond.
"Hello, frog! Will you play with me?"

"Sure! Let's hop," croaked the frog,
as he hopped onto a lily pad
in the middle of a pond.

Patrick tried to follow. He hopped
as hard as he could, but . . .

Oops!

Patrick shook himself off and looked around
for the frog. But the frog was gone.

Then Patrick saw a white cat sitting on a wall. "Hello, cat! Will you play with me?"

"Yikes! A dog!" yowled the cat
as she ran away.

"Doesn't *anyone* want to play with me?"
he sniffed, when . . .

a little boy came out of the house. "Patrick!
Will you play with me?" called the boy.

Patrick wagged his tail. The boy grinned.
"Good. Let's race!"

Patrick and the boy ran and ran. They played
fetch the stick and catch the ball.

They turned somersaults
in the warm, tickly grass.

"I'm glad I have you to play with," said the boy. "I'm glad I have *you!*" Patrick barked.

All tuckered out, the two playmates went
back inside, curled up, and took
a nice, long nap!